T0162650

THE BOTTLED Wind

IKE MORAH

authorHOUSE®

AuthorHouse™
1663 Liberty Drive
Bloomington, IN 47403
www.authorhouse.com
Phone: 1-800-839-8640

Published by AuthorHouse   06/22/2012

ISBN: 978-1-4772-2878-4 (sc)
ISBN: 978-1-4772-2879-1 (e)

Library of Congress Control Number: 2012911338

It had been a whirlwind romance between Johnny Cash and Joy, alias Ngozi. Now they are man and wife as Mr. & Mrs. J. J. Cash.

Johnny had called back to his office to ask for a few more days extra to be added to his leave since they were preparing to take off on a honeymoon. They had been in too much of a hurry and so there had been no time at all for courtship or wooing, as he preferred to call it. Though this was not exactly necessary, they had decided to make it a memorable honeymoon in order to make up for that deficiency. They had already done more than enough, but they just wanted it to be there for the records.

The wedding had taken place in the Bishops court as promised and planned, and they were back to the hotel. The Bishop had officiated and he was the only other witness to the ceremony. No one else in town knew what had taken place there in the house.

When they got home, they were very happy, and they slept through the day. It was only when they awoke in the evening that they decided on their first act together as man and wife.

Their first assignment was to visit a film theater. Joy was a veteran of film theaters, but as for Johnny, he had never been to one. Watching films at home had hitherto contented him. This was however going to be a new experience since it was what would have been expected of dating couples.

They had bought a late evening newspaper, but it was only to check out its entertainment section. It was from there that they learnt that there were four film theaters in that town. They checked out the films advertised for each and finally settled for the 'Aristocrat Theater'. The film for that evening seemed to be the reverse adaptation of one that she had watched before. That was Lady Chatterley's lover, and this one was 'Tom Brown's lover'.

They were there rather early, but the idea was to familiarize themselves with the place. They had a double martini at the bar just across the road from the theater before going in. At the lobby to the theater they bought a bucket of popcorns as well as a couple of non-alcoholic Champaign. It was not yet time to start, and so the interior of the theater itself was still brightly lit. It was a very special theater, which was built in the era when they had a king.

They had paid for one of the honeymoon seats. These were a pair of cozy seats on either side of the projection window. They were therefore located higher up than all the other seats. In earlier times, the queen and the king used to seat on one side while the heir apparent to the throne sat on the other pair with his wife, girl friend or whoever he wished. That was before the era of DVDS and other home entertainment systems.

They were therefore very luxurious seats and each cost about five times as much as the other seats, but they were worth it. They were private and there was not going to be even the slightest disturbance from those who wanted to move out or in as they watched the films. In fact, each side had its own private rest room, just for the couple. They were located just besides them. They did not however fail to notice that the couple who came to sit on the other side was the cities Mayor. The Mayor was a lady, and from what they noticed, her partner did not seem to be her husband. Joy had seen their photograph before and she did not fail to comment on that. It was much later that they found out that her partner was one of the contractors that patronized the city government. Politicians were very often like that.

Joy was dressed in such a way that one would not be wrong to say that she was dressed to kill. At the ticketing counter, the clerk had made a remark to the effect that he was not aware of the fact that aristocrats were still around. He was sure that they were royalty. She looked stunningly pretty in the flimsy mauve blouse that he had just purchased for her the previous day. The clerk had mumbled something to the effect that she was the prettiest damsel that he had ever set eyes on in the entire fifty years that he had been on earth.

She was in that mauve chiffon blouse with a moderately low neckline. He did not want anything that would be low enough to make others share her beauty with him. He was already getting possessive. The mid-length black pleated skirt that complimented the blouse was made from worsted Llama wool, and it was sown to fit. Both the blouse and the skirt seemed to jealously hug her body while accentuating all her curves. The skirt made her derriere seem particularly obvious. Her leggings were of a rare light gray color, but it was her shoes that told the entire story. They made people look twice and downwards. They were pointed stilettos with moderate heels crafted from suckling seal leather. They were therefore very soft and able to take in and enhance the blackness of the tanning color. It was therefore of a very rare shade of black with a most intriguing shape.

Her hat was the type that one would not be wrong to describe as a royal hat. It was a rather small sized sombrero design hat that was made out of stiffened silk netting. The rims and perimeter were stiffened with peacock feathers and that made it look particularly beautiful. The ribbon at the base of the hat was tied in a perfect bow that was the same color with her blouse, and it was sort of heavenly to behold.

A single ten-karat emerald stud set in twenty-four karat yellow gold decorated either ear. This was a perfect complement to her gold ladies Rolex wristwatch. The wedding ring that Johnny had bought was also one of a kind. It was meant just for dressing and not for everyday wearing. It was an eight hundred dollar ring. It was made of twenty-four karat yellow gold inlaid with twenty karats of fiery green emerald. Johnny had chosen twenty-four karat gold for all the jewelry that he bought for her because he had insisted that it was the only thing that was as pure as she looked. She was probably not pure in spirit but at least she looked so, moreover he had agreed to let bygones be bygones.

Now back to the film theater. It was not quite long after they had taken their seat that the lights began to dim. It was time for the coming attractions and other advertisements. It was only during this period that most veterans of the film theater began to come in. It was a little bit rowdy below as they milled around in all directions, looking for seats at vantage positions. Finally the lights went off and the main attraction started right away.

It was a very slow paced romantic film without too many characters. It was a film set around an aristocratic family. Lady Isabella had married her cousin, John Doe, not because she was madly in love with him or even in love with him at all, but it was for two selfish reasons. First of all she wanted the wealth from their great grand parents to remain in the family. Secondly, and more importantly however, was the fact that she was a prude. She was not just a prude, she was homophobic and yet she was not a lesbian. It was claimed that she even hated women more than she hated men. The fact that she was related to John would make sure that they will not be exactly attracted to each other, at least physically. That would be contrary to the natural order of things.

They lived alone in a very big mansion and he was not exactly fulfilled as he had put it. Though she did not love him, she was very jealous of any other female who talked to him, and that was particularly obvious when they went out for occasional parties. She was very pretty and he was very handsome. They lived together and yet they lived apart. It was because of the money that he did not mind living that life. He was free to escape the marriage and live a more fulfilled life, but then the money would not be there if he did so.

They were each still way below their middle age, but they had a housemaid who was a woman well beyond what one might consider an advanced age. She was not pretty, no matter how one looked at it, but she carried herself very well. She was therefore an old lady who was at least more that forty years older than either of them. She was a widow. She lived in a single room hut that was built for her just outside the rear wall and small gate of the mansion. Beyond there was a vast forest, which incidentally belonged to them too.

One faithful day, while the lady of the house was having her bath, the maid came in to drop off her clothing that she had picked up from the dry cleaners place. She had forgotten to check for their mail and so she decided to keep the clothes in the outer room and go back for the mails. She remembered seeing the mailman dropping off some mails as she came in. She came in just as John was about to dress up. He was completely naked when she came in. She was shocked and tried to apologize as she turned away her eyes:

"I am terribly sorry sir." She had said this in a very shy tone and she was afraid.

"Why?"

"For coming in at the wrong time without knocking." She was beginning to walk back to the door.

"Hold on!" He ordered, and she stopped in her tracks totally confused. He however continued:

"Why are you turning away?"

"Because I should not see you naked."

"Why not?"

"You are my boss."

"But what would you have done if I were your lover?"

"I guess I might not turn away."

"In that case I want you to pretend that I am your lover."

"But I can't."

"Why?"

"I don't know, but all I know is that it would be impossible for me to imagine that."

By this time he had stealthily come very close to her while she was still facing away. He knew that his wife was still in the bathroom, but that did not matter. It was always a two-hour ritual and she had been there for only thirty minutes. In other words, he did not really have to worry about her and the maid was also aware of that fact. She always took her time there.

He then touched her on the shoulder and she flinched. This was not because she did not want him. She did not even think of that at all, but it was because she was surprised. He did not want to waste time and so he went right ahead to introduce what was going on in his mind.

"Do you know that at times I wish you were my lover?" She did not answer. She just stood there looking away and refusing to turn around. She was too confused to comprehend what was going on. More over she hardly believed her ears. He was handsome and she was ugly. He was young and she was very old. He was rich and she was pathetically poor. The gap between them was not just a gap, it was a chasm. To make matters worse, she had always known him as a quiet and perfect gentleman. Maybe, that goes to prove that the saying that a gentleman is just a man who has not yet been caught in the act. He however continued with his suggestions:

"Do you ever have the feeling to make love?" She swallowed very hard before lying:

"No."

"Don't forget that I am your boss, so tell me the truth."

"At times."

"Do you have any lover?"

"No."

"In that case you are about to get one. I will see you tomorrow by midmorning."

"But by mid morning I am off and in my hut."

"I am very much aware of that. I will visit you."

"But what of your wife?"

"Don't worry yourself about that. I will take care of her. When I come in, I will tell you what I have done to keep her away. See you tomorrow."

She walked out still confused. She was not too sure that it was going to be true but she was expectantly happy at that possibility. She completed her chores for the rest of the day making every effort to keep away from wherever he was, and whenever that was not possible, she would make it short. She also made sure that she never looked directly at him, and he did not fail to notice that.

Immediately after she left, he hatched out a master plan that would place him around her hut the following day by midmorning. Immediately Isabella came out from the bathroom, he informed her that he was rushing in and out of town to buy something. It was going to take him less than twenty minutes. She knew that twenty minutes would not be enough for any hanky—panky business and so she did not mind.

A few minutes sooner than she had expected, he came back. He had acquired a hunting rifle together with hunting boots. He then went on to inform her that he was about to take up hunting as a hobby. She was excited about that prospect. The reason was that it meant that he would be away to the forest for some hours daily, or at least quite often, without her having to worry about where he was. It is not that she would worry about his safety or something like that, but it meant that he was not with another lady.

"When are you starting?" She asked in her usually very deceptively calm voice.

"I guess tomorrow will be alright."

"Why not this evening?"

"I was hoping to go after those pheasants, but they seem to be at their most vulnerable by midmorning. That's why I thought of starting tomorrow."

"That's a good idea, but I didn't know that you were a good hunter."

"I was before, but I believe that I have lost my touch. I guess it will take some time before I become perfect at shooting once more."

"I wish you lots of luck."

"Thanks my dear."

"I believe this calls for a drink."

"That is perfectly in order."

It was John that went to fetch the drinks. Her favorite was Martini Rossi, and they had quite more than a few bottles of it around.

Just after midmorning the following day, John Doe left the mansion through the small rear gate. He was in his hunting boots with his rifle slung over his shoulder. He was dressed for the hunt.

As soon as he cleared the small gate, he looked around to make sure that no one was looking at or saw him. He then veered to the nearby small hut and tapped timidly on the door. There was no answer, but he could hear her footsteps in the hut. When the footsteps got to the door he heard a very low voice ask:

"Who is it?"

"It's me." That was the reply. Under normal conditions that would not be a valid answer to that question, but she recognized the voice. She quietly and quickly opened the door and he immediately slipped in as she hurriedly closed it behind her. She then locked it and finally latched it shut.

He put down his gun in one corner of the room while taking in everything that was there. There wasn't really much to take in. It was just a single bed, a center table and a sofa, with some cooking utensils in one corner. He was moved into pity when he realized that she was living there as a destitute and yet she was serving them.

He sat down on the sofa and pulled off his hunting boots before saying anything:

"That's a nice and neat room, though it is rather too small."

"It's that simple because I don't have much property."

"I like it."

"Thanks."

"I don't really know much about you."

"What would you like to know?"

"Everything."

"Okay, I am from Inverness Heights. My husband died about fifteen years ago and we had no child. That's why I live alone."

"What of relatives?"

"None whatsoever."

"Not even an uncle or so?"

"None at all. I was an orphan."

"I see."

"Can I offer you anything to drink sir?"

"Please cut off the sir. I am not thirsty so don't worry about that, but thanks anyway."

"It's your first time here and I feel obliged to offer you something."

"But you know what I want."

That was enough to make her nervous. She sat by the foot of the bed looking rather nervous and began to look away from him. This was one of those situations that never failed to baffle him. From how she was dressed, she must have been longing for him and was obviously waiting for him and yet she was nervous, and he would not be surprised if she protested. He then got up from the sofa, went over to her and just stood in front of her. She looked further away.

He then gingerly reached for her hands, held them and tried to make her stand up. Rather than resist as he had expected, she sort of got up on her own, though slowly while still looking away. He held her close to himself and she remained motionless. To him, that was a very good sign indeed. Everything seemed to be working according to plan. He then took those arms and put them around his neck. She let them remain there and he noticed that she actually got them tighter than he had put them. He gave her a fleeting kiss on her cheek without any noticeable response.

There were a few other maneuvers, each of which pointed to her willingness, and so he proceeded to undress her. When she did not resist he attributed it to either that she was eager to be a willing participant or that she was afraid to offend her boss. Rather than resist, she actually helped him do so. Within seconds, even his own clothes were on the floor as well. Her breasts were hanging down, but he did not mind. He tried to play with them for a while before turning her around so that he was at her back. He then let his right hand drop down to that area between her legs, she took one leg up to the bed to open up a little bit better.

He rummaged through the bush that was there for she had not thought of clearing them in a long time. It was literarily a thick bush. As soon as he was able to part some of the hair and get his fingers onto something more reasonable, she flinched. It was only then that he got convinced that she was alive. It had been a long time, maybe as long as the many years that she had been a widow, that someone tried to get to that area. It was obvious that she was ready for him and had been itching for this, not minding that thick mat of hair. He caressed, rubbed and probed in and around that territory and she moaned without stopping. It was only then that he gradually let her down on to the bed. He parted her legs, though she was already doing so before his help. He only did that in order to be able to figure out what to do with that thick forest of hair there. He was aware of how brutal these hairs could be. They could lacerate any mans organ without mercy and he was not ready for that. They could at times be much sharper than razor blades.

He eventually succeeded in parting the bush to either side. They were already very wet. He could not wait as he inserted his manhood into her yearning caverns. He had not finished inserting it when she opened her legs even more widely while kicking wildly in the air. It was not long before they both climaxed. He came down from the bed and began to dress up.

"Thank you very much." That was all that came out of her as she lay down there on the bed. She was savoring the experience.

"For what?" He asked.

"For making me to remember once more that I am still a woman."

"Would you mind if I came again another day?"

"No. I will not mind at all. In fact you are more than welcome."

As soon as he was fully dressed up, he stole out of the hut. He went further down and took a shot into the air for the records. It was not long after that before he made it to their mansion.

"Hello darling, were you able to bag any game? I heard your shot."

"I only came across one and I missed. It was not encouraging."

"Oh, poor you. Maybe you'll have better luck next time."

"I believe so, after all it is claimed that practice makes perfect. I hope to net in one very soon."

"I wish you luck."

"Thanks."

With that he went in for a very hot bath having been very fulfilled.

This went on for some time before a near misfortune made them change venue for their trysts, or at least that was what the film suggested. It was not a misfortune as such; it was just a scare.

One day, he was there as usual and had just finished undressing when a knock came on the door of the hut. They both got alarmed. She had never had any visitor there except for him. Before she could finish asking who it was, her voice rang out. It was the lady of the house:

"Please could you come and help me find my pink evening dress. I wasn't sure of where it was. Do you know?"

"Yes my lady. I saw it just this morning."

"Would you come then?"

"Of course, I will come after you."

"Don't mind, I'll wait for you here."

As soon as her husband heard her voice, he dived under the bed, and then out again to collect his belongings before diving back under. It was funny, but the maid could not laugh. He was still naked. The maid, apart from his bedmatic antics, did not know that her boss could be so athletic.

By the time she opened the door to attend to her Ladyship, she was already fully dressed. She simply slammed the door behind her as if she was in a hurry and followed her.

"Why don't you go back and lock your door?"

"I guess that any thief that decides to go there will go back home at a loss. There will be nothing worthwhile to steal."

They both laughed about that comment before she added:

"I insist, one can never tell."

She usually locked the door from outside with a padlock, but she had left it inside the house. As soon as she opened the door, she tried to grab it and back out, but her boss was already peeping through the door.

"What a nice neat little room you have here."

"Thanks." She was very nervous and afraid that she might discover their secret, but fortunately, her lover was still under the bed, but he could clearly see them from there. He was trying his very best to see how to convince the earth to open up and swallow him. He was lucky. His wife had just missed him by a mere hairbreadth.

They locked the door behind them and took off. As for himself, he dressed up and let himself out of the back window into the forest, closing it behind him.

That near incidence was enough to make him think twice. The film ended there while they were thinking of the next and safer place to use. No one was sure of what followed.

By the time people left the theatre it was all laughs and discussions. Some wanted to see more. Some felt that his wife pressured the man into breaking his marital vows and so they could not blame him. Some blamed the old maid. Some blamed Isabella since she was the person who put her husband in that situation. Some blamed him. This was the set that felt that if reverend fathers could abstain, at least in theory, then he could too; after all, he opted for it. There was more than enough blame to go around, and of course there were always those who disagreed with each of those views.

When they got home, Johnny and Joy tried to remember parts of the film, but they seemed to have been more interested in what took place in that hut.

Early the following morning, while she was still asleep, Johnny stole out to the lobby. He had secretly paid a florist to deliver some flowers very early in the morning to the hotel. He was to leave them with the receptionist for him. They were roses.

Joy was thirty years old and so he had decided to give her thirty roses for each of the decades of her life. He had arranged with, and paid the florist to deliver them to the receptionist very early in the morning. They were there and the entire lobby smelt of roses. He wanted to carry them up himself so as not to disturb her or wake her up.

The roses were arranged as he had requested. There were thirty white roses, thirty pink ones and thirty deep red velvet ones. They were all of the most fragrant varieties. They were all still very fresh and were just about to open up fully.

When he got to their room, he quietly laid them on the center table and went back to bed. He made sure that the lights were off and pretended to be fast asleep while waiting for when she will wake up.

Suddenly she poked him by the ribs and asked:

"Do you smell roses everywhere?"

"No."

"That means that I am dreaming."

"I guess so."

There was a lull and she tried to pinch herself to make sure that she was not really asleep. She was convinced that she was not asleep, but one could never tell. She then poked him once more, but this time around it was with a request:

"Darling, could you please help me put on the lights?"

"Men, I don't want it to disturb my sweet dreams."

"Which dreams are you in?"

"I was just dreaming about you."

"What about?"

"But you know."

"Tell me what exactly happened in the dream."

"But you know."

"How should I know?"

"But you were there."

"What does that mean?"

"We were together in the dream and I can remember all the things you said in it, so how could I remember all the things you said and you can't?"

"When was that?"

"I was still in it when you started talking about putting on the lights."

It was then that she realized that he was only joking. She therefore hit him lightly on the back and said while laughing:

"You liar."

"But I am not lying."

"If you are not, how are you able to be in a dream and yet be able to answer my questions?"

"That is because both my mouth and ears were already awake, but my brain was still somewhere in dreamland."

"Now that you are awake, do you smell the roses?"

"Yes, I do."

"Where could those nice fragrances be coming from?"

"My guess is that they are wafting in from the balcony."

"Switch on the light then lets go and take a look."

"Okay baby."

The light switch was just on the leg of the bed on his side. He did not have to get up to switch it on. As soon as he put it on she shouted:

"Oh my God!" The roses stunned her. They were many and she was still trying to figure out how they came to be there. They were a spectacle to behold as she ran out of bed to take a closer look at them. They were arranged in a triangle with one color on each side. There was a bottle of a very rare vintage Champaign at each corner.

As she got there, she bent over to further savor that heavenly smell of the roses and then noticed that there was an envelope in the middle of it. She took it because it was addressed to her—Mrs. J Cash. When she opened it, there was just a piece of paper in it. Only one sentence was scribbled there in a handwriting that she had now come to recognize.

"To the one I love, a belated courtship gesture."

It was propped up with a bottle of perfume. It was the largest size of channel five perfume that she had ever seen. It was her favorite and it was of course within the expensive bracket. She was excited as she opened it and dabbed a little bit behind her ears and on her neck while glancing backwards. He was still pretending to be asleep. She knew that she had been madly in love with him, but were there any other thing stronger than love then she was in whatever it was, there and then. Her emotions had been taken over by passion as she began to get teary without knowing why. She could not discern her feelings. They were tears of happiness.

She then approached her man on the bed. She did so looking very innocent and deceptively shy. He was aware of the fact that she was in love and he had been watching her surreptitiously. He did not allow her get to the bed before he got up.

"I love you Johnny."

That was all that she could say, and before he could reply, she shut him up with one of those her patented kisses. Her lips were fairly well endowed and they always looked wet though never wet. He preferred to consider them as a very juicy pair. Her lips had entirely covered his mouth while her tongue parted his own lips before he could open them. With it she searched frantically within his mouth while sucking away. That was more than enough to put him on fire. There was a brand of battery named Eveready and she thought of her man as Eveready.

They were both on fire as he gingerly lifted her up and then put her back on the bed. The strong perfume of the roses seemed to sort of act as an aphrodisiac. They were each in a hurry to get it going.

She feverishly managed to get her negligee off and to the floor, but as for him, his pajamas seemed to have mysteriously vanished from his body and fallen to the floor too. They were both ready for action. He held on to her breasts as if they were the only things that would prevent him from falling to the floor, but then he went on to suck enthusiastically at her nipples. This was a ritual that he insisted that he always did to compensate for having missed breast-feeding as a child. He was raised solely on infant formula. It was his opportunity to make up for that loss. The important thing is that they both enjoyed it, though she probably enjoyed it more than he did.

While that was going on, she was also hanging on to his manhood with both palms. It was erect and as strong as a metal rod. She shuddered as she imagined what that was going to do to her later. He was actually slightly more than well endowed and she loved it. It was just a perfect fit for her.

She moaned softly once in a while, but it was not till one of his hands relocated to somewhere lower down that she got really fired up. As soon as his fingers got to between her legs, she shuddered while opening up. Her hands shot up and held tight to the bedposts as he touched her sensitive area. She moaned loudly and pleaded for him to go in. Who was he not to obey?

With shaky hands, he steadily and cautiously let himself into her. She stiffened more and began to shudder wildly with every muscle tightening uncontrollably. She was wet all over both inside and outside while sweating. He was surprised as to how fast things were going. He was already in space or the other world when he felt her tightening up around him.

Before he could contemplate what was happening, they both shouted in Unisom. They had climaxed as they grabbed and gripped each other with reckless abandon. Each seemed to be struggling to squeeze out the last drop from the other. They lay there on their backs looking at each other and unable to talk. They were wondering how fast and spontaneously it had come, as well as how fast it had all ended. They were panting and they were exhausted.

It was only about two hours latter that they realized that they had fallen asleep. That was when they awoke. They both woke up at the same time. They were both fully refreshed as they went in, one after the other, for an early morning hot bath. It was then time for breakfast and they were ravenously hungry. It was not as early as one would think and so they headed for the 'seaman's eatery'.

It was going to be a combination of late breakfast and early lunch—a brunch to be specific. It was for this reason that this particular restaurant does not have a menu at all during this period. Every order had to be a la carte.

Seaman's eatery was a very exclusive restaurant, and it was situated right at the entrance of the bay. It was considered exclusive in that most of their dinning rooms were built for two.

When they got there, they opted for valet parking and then booked for one of the rooms upstairs. From there they could look down on the fishing trawlers and boats that were moving in and out of the bay. As soon as they settled down, a server came in and offered them a list. Rather than a menu, they were offered a list of available ingredients and it was for them to choose what they wanted to be created for them.

After going through the list they went for Live Lobster tails, Live Salmon, Oysters, Cauliflower, Spinach, tomatoes, beets, romaine lettuce with a few other vegetables. After that, it would take the chefs about half an hour to create something out of the chosen ingredients.

As an appetizer, they opted for chunky chicken soup with rye bread. This was washed down with the costliest and rarest vintage they had there. It was a one hundred and twenty year old Grand Rosemary red wine. It had been in their cellar under the building for many years and no one had ever dared spend the money that was their asking price for it. It was claimed to have been fermented with grapes that had come from the foothills of mount Etna in the era prior to the First World War. This was some three years after one of its numerous volcanic eruptions. It was claimed that the volcanic ash on which it was grown had given that year's vintage from there a very unique flavor. It seemed as if this bottle had been patiently waiting for this very occasion.

The wine arrived in a gold plated silver tray reserved for such occasions. The butler brought it in, handling it as gingerly as he could. He presented it to them, before opening it. As soon as the cork yielded, its sophisticated aroma filled the room. Nonetheless they were each offered a little bit of it for the tasting.

It was a deep red color, which suggested that it was a heavy wine. This type had always been their favorite.

Joy gently swirled her own in her hand before slowly passing the glass very close to her nostrils. With her eyes closed, she breathed in deeply as the glass crossed. She inhaled that aroma and then exhaled as she opened her eyes with a look of total satisfaction on her face. As the aroma tickled her nostrils, she realized that the bouquet had a very distinctive character. It was a totally heavenly aromatic experience. The character that it exuded was complex as well as woody, but it was all the same well integrated. It was a totally harmonized blend and fusion of characters. She then took a small sip, swirled it round in her mouth, let it settle there for a few seconds with out disturbance and then swallowed it.

She was paying attention and listening to each and all of her taste buds as well as her organs of smell. As to the feel or expressiveness, its texture and weight as well as structure and flavor, it pointed to a perfectly harmonized product. The after-taste suggested that the aging was also perfect.

It was a well-aged wine and she could even detect the very faint contribution from the oak barrel where it used to be. Her final opinion was that it had come as a heavy well-aged heavy wine from Pinot Noir grapes. It was rare and it had been served as a full-bodied red wine at the perfect temperature of sixty-one degrees Fahrenheit.

She finally opened her eyes, smiled with satisfaction and presented her glass to the butler for some more. Johnny was not exactly into wines. He took it that she had decided for both of them and so for him, it was down the hatch, as he presented his own glass too. Of course he was right. They were now united into one, one for two and two for one. They settled down to drink the wine while chattering about the weather, the restaurant and of course about that rarest of all vintages.

Exactly thirty minutes later the main course arrived. It was presented in a very mouthwatering fashion. It was claimed that it is the eyes that eat first before the rest of the man. This saying was definitely true.

The romaine lettuce was used as a carpet on which the rest were presented. Every other thing was in the plate, together and yet separate from each other. Only the oyster was presented alone. They came in two small oyster servers with paring knives in them.

On one side of the dish was the white cauliflower decorated with purple arctic tomatoes in decorative slices. On the opposite side was a giant Lobster tail fried to a perfect orange color in extra virgin olive oil. The wedges of Salmon were gingerly balanced next to the tail. They could not tell what spices were used but they smelt heavenly. The fragrance from the mixture of spices alone was enough to make them very hungry. They could not wait as they fell on the food like a pair of hungry wolves, not being too sure of where to start.

It tasted even better than it both looked and smelt. By the time they finished, they were each sure that it was the best seafood meal they had ever had.

Finally the dessert was presented. It was Grand Ma's Apple pie, and it was her favorite pie. It was topped with nonfat Greek style Yogurt. This was washed down with brandy. It was another rare vintage of Napoleon VSOP Brandy.

They had eaten more than they should have, and the Brandy did not help matters. They felt very heavy and maybe a little bit lazy from the overfeeding aided by the effect of the Brandy. They rested for almost an hour before taking off. Once outside they went to the harbor and sat down on one of the benches to give the food time to digest further. It was a much-needed rest considering the fact that they had overfed themselves.

This particular area of the harbor was called the love garden and it was while they were there that they found out how that name came to be. There were many couples strolling around and it was obvious that they were lovers. Besides, and around where they had the benches, were many flower beds and they were well tended and bloomed all year round. There were many visitors there and they ate a lot of snacks while idling around and taking photographs. Opportunistic photographers were everywhere and they were making brisk business.

One of the photographers had offered his services and they accepted. It was a fast one, and in less than six minutes he was back with some copies of their picture. It was taken under the backdrop of the city skyline and the sky as background. It was very clear and the color fantastic. They looked like a royal couple that had just come into town. They paid for a few copies as well as for an enlargement.

There were many birds flying about there, but the most numerous were the sea gulls. They were everywhere and they made a lot of noise. Once in a while there would be a frantic rush amongst them as they dash off to a far away fishing boat. They later found out that those were boats that were cleaning out a little way off the bay, and they were headed there for some washed off bits of fish.

A couple of ravens tended to hang around these sea gulls, usually in order to try and steal some of their food. One interesting thing that they noted was however the fact that they had now adapted to human cuisine. Many of them would rather go for fast food. Whatever food was thrown away was immediately attended to. They would dive down and struggle for, as well as fight for the food.

There are always all sorts of characters in every society. There were the good and there were the bad. Amongst these birds were thieves and robbers too. One funny incident was when one lady just came out of a fast food store with a load of food that she had just bought for her family. Three ravens suddenly swooped down and went on the attack. It was a well-coordinated attack. One of them tried to distract her attention by flying and flapping its wings on her face. She dropped the food in order to shield her face. They immediately made off with the bag of food.

The harbor police who witnessed the episode started off laughing at the incidence before running over to help the lady. Joy on her part laughed so much that her ribs started paining her. She ended up by jokingly asking Johnny what he thought those police men were going to charge the ravens for. She was not sure if it was going to be for burglary or for robbery, and if robbery would it be armed or not?

Had it been a man or some men that did the same thing, they would have gone after him right away. That looked like discrimination to her. For the lady, it was no laughing matter. She eventually tried to chase after them, but the raven is a very intelligent bird. As soon as it became obvious to them that she was about to go after them, they carried their loot together and flew over to the other side of the harbor, as people watched in amusement.

Johnny and Joy sat there for well over an hour holding tight to each other as if they were afraid that someone might steal one of them. When they got tired, they headed for the car parking lot and the valet on sighting them brought out their car. The wind had essentially died down and it was now a very mild breeze. As they went on, his mind was still going through two poems that he had once read. One was the becalming wind and the other was the breathe of the gods.

Becalming Wind

By day or night without a choice,
Like ghosts in poltergy it fans its way
Lifting strands from tattered roofs.
Light enough it often stirs the lake
Tracing shimmers on its languid top
As if some fleet-footed water roach
Had hover-raced on her placid surface.
Like some invisible breathe
It fans some diverse fancied amber
Like some invisible heavenly hand
As it swirls dry resting leaves
Her invisible fingers tracing on the sands
Ephemeral patterns that come and go.
Often through seemingly eloquent stillness
It whispers through the boughs—
Rich in imagined transient words—
Oftener whispering to passers by
And gossiping of others gone by.
Its thrilling hushes like some mists
Hang both high and low over the vale
As it does the imagination haunt
For love and passion to ensnare.

Breath Of The Gods

Breath of the gods often quite unseen
Like ghosts fleeing an enchanters wand
Chariot their whims across to us.
These spirit beings becalm at will
Surging around in mournful dirge—
Slumbery as if waking from evaporating frills—
Their clarion calls—this loathsome dirge:
Uncontrolled sounds of fear that
Swiftly and timelessly rustle the leaves—
Tumultuous evidence of spirits brisk but fierce.
Like resurrections that control awakenings.
Leaves and blades in prayer bow with fear
As cry the skies at what they saw.
These indiscretions are calmed to hushy wisps,
Her powers tamed all at once
Its fierceness tempered by the pleading tears
As this hushy breath of the gods
Is felt but rather unseen.

That was how the winds had played on them that afternoon. It was light when they came out and it had come to be almost still, while the clouds darkened. A few showers had come and gone and it was time for them to go too. These were poems that he had read before, or more probably they had come to him as inspirations.

They entered their car and drove back to the hotel.

What eventually went on in the hotel is best left to the imagination, but they had decided on a road trip the following morning.

The road trip was however postponed because she had pointed out that the first Sunday after a wedding was supposed to be recognized. They therefore decided to dedicate that day to the church.

On Saturday evening they thought of which church to attend. It did not really matter which it was to any of them. All that mattered is that it should be a Christian church. They each simply believed in Christianity and nothing more. Johnny had some reservations about a few of them and she had her own too, but they were ready to head into whichever one they came across.

They were still discussing this issue about Christianity, churches and which one to attend and this was how it went when Joy had started off:

"Darling?" She called out.

"Yes?" Answered Johnny.

"Can we go to church tomorrow?"

"What for?"

"The first Sunday after a private wedding should surely be devoted to the Lord. I would love to at least thank him for making me see you and for letting us get hitched."

"Please don't count me out. It will be very inconsiderate of me not to do the same."

"Just because I wanted to do so?"

"No. Not for that. I have been thinking of what miracles the Lord had performed for me within these last few days."

"Which miracles?"

"I managed to catch up with you for starters."

"That's a miracle quite all right."

"Apart from that, everything seems to have happened very smoothly and perfectly well too."

"As for myself, at times I still feel puzzled at how fast everything had gone. At times I even don't quite believe it. It occasionally feels as if I am working in Limbo."

"Do you recall when I was pouring ice-cold water over my head in the morning?"

"Yes. Was that not when I was trying to find out if you had headache?"

"Exactly. I was only trying to call myself back to my senses, in order to make sure that this was all for real."

It took them well over thirty minutes to lay to rest the issue of how surprised, satisfied and happy they felt about having found each other all through to the wedding. Finally came the issue of which church to attend:

"Do you know one funny thing?" Johnny asked.

"No, what?"

"I was born into a protestant family, but I was in that church last some six years ago."

"Why?"

"I stopped going there when, though the bible was clearly against homosexual practices, an openly gay member of the clergy was elevated and consecrated a bishop."

"I heard of that and it puzzled and pained me to my bones."

"To add salt to injury, the now consecrated bishop went right ahead to wed his partner in the church."

"I was not aware of that part of the saga."

"Sure he did. They had been together for well over ten years before then. Call it fornication and you will be wrong technically. He had put out his wife, though they were not exactly in favor of divorce, and got him in as his live-in lover."

"Does that not constitute a direct or frontal attack on God?"

"It is. But if angels could revolt against Him, who are humans not to?"

"You have a point there. If I remember correctly, it was a revolt by a group of angels against Him that led to Lucifer becoming the Satan."

"You are right on the point."

"But don't you think that one could just ignore him and go ahead with worshiping God there. He was just an individual, though a bad one at that, and there are bound to be many good ones."

"I don't quite see it that way."

"Have you forgotten when you mentioned the popular injunction: 'do as I say and not as I do'?"

"I remember that very well, but don't forget that we are also supposed to live and learn by examples."

"I agree with you there, but remember that one has the option and freewill to live by either the good examples or the bad ones."

"Haven't you come across that saying out of Africa which goes like this; 'when one finger touches the oil, it spreads to the rest'. In other words, when one priest does something bad, it spreads to the rest. To me, prevention is better than cure. I figured that it was time for me to check out of there."

"Do you realize that you are not the only person who has had reservations about a church?"

"You do too?"

"I was born Catholic—Roman Catholic to be precise. Incidentally my father was a Revered Father."

"Hold it Joy. Are Reverend Fathers not celibate?"

"In theory? Yes they are. But in practice many of them are not. In fact most of them are not exactly celibate. They are just bachelors."

"How did that go with your father?"

"Directly after his consecration, he officially announced that he was sponsoring his fathers marriage to a young girl. This was just after his mother's death. It was all a cover up. That was how he married my mother. She was his wife, but lived at home in my grandfather's house. He had us, five of us."

"That's one heck of a reverend father! I doff my hat for him! But don't you think that it was bad?"

"When we grew up and managed to accuse him of that, he insisted that at least he had some conscience. He never failed to remind us of our family friend, Mr. and Mrs. Smith. Both mister Smith and Bianca, his wife, were in Rome at the same time. Mr. Smith was then in his final year in the seminary in the Vatican while Bianca was a reverend sister there too. Bianca however managed to get pregnant for him and so they were both kicked out of the church. It all happened under the Pope's nose as it were."

"I have heard of such before, but I thought that it was just one of those stories."

"There were even worse instances."

"I don't think any other act could be worse than that of those two."

"That's nothing. Reverend Father John Bull used to be in the same parish as my father. One male member of his congregation once came to complain to him that his wife was cheating on him. When he asked if he had any concrete evidence, the man said that he was very sure of what he was saying but that if it came to catching her openly he had not. John bull started bringing them in for marriage counseling and this lasted a little bit over a year. His wife took in and the man insisted that it was not his child. After childbirth they went for paternity test. Guess who was the father?"

"He himself, or maybe his closest friend."

"No. It was John Bull himself. He had been the culprit all along even before the counseling episodes."

"What happened after that?"

"The marriage was annulled and John Bull was reassigned to Rome for special duties."

"Please don't tell me that you have more of such stories."

"Of course there are more, even more juicy ones."

"Please stop. I don't want to hear more. They might make me opt out of Christianity altogether."

"In fact the only thing that had kept me in that fold is that idea of: 'don't ask don't tell'. Some will try to put it this way: what one does not know will not kill him."

"In that case what we have to do tomorrow is to go out and enter any building we see as a Christian church irrespective of the denomination."

"Okay then."

"Incidentally I was told that in the next town which is not far from here, they have the equivalent of a church mall."

"What does that mean?"

"Its like malls in which only churches are allowed to rent the units. I was told that they have well over ten Christian churches there together with three mystical churches, two mosques and a satanic church."

"I am just wondering what they will call such a mall."

"It is the Landover Religious Mall. Their motto is: "Freedom of worship". Because of this motto, there is a quasi-religious sect that worships in one of the hallways.

They simply worship, without worshipping anything in particular."

"If I may ask, how do you come by all this information?"

"You don't believe me?"

"How dare you ask that? I believe you completely."

"Okay. It seems that you have forgotten that I have always been an insider. My father was in it, and my former boyfriend, or sugar-daddy however you look at him, was in it too."

"You must be a working encyclopedia."

"That's me."

It was a relatively uneventful evening and so they had to wait for the following morning before they took off to the religious mall.

When they got to the parking lot, she opted for a drive-in church. In this particular one, all they had to do was to drive in to a designated area and park. The preacher would then climb a table by his own car and conduct the service from there.

Johnny was impressed and it was while they were there that he wrote down what he experienced there in the form of a poem. They had come in a little bit late, and most of the churches were already half way through. There were songs from every corner and he was so carried away by these that he had to write about them while the pastor was ranting away. It was the 'symphony of celestial songs'.

The Symphony Of
Celestial Songs

The notes came floating undressed
Into ears that never really cared.
At times they came in undressed
To draw attention to those that sing.

Through space they float and come
Fully lulled to trick the ears
From angelic throats that seem to come
Fully charged to calm our thoughts.

Like sleeping aid from a doctor's pad
Penned to lull to internal bliss;
Or as pills from the Pharmacist's bag
They beckon us to blissful dreamland.

Sounds of wonder songs of praise
Oft in tones that kiss the ears
There they come to enslave and raise
Those voices to the Lord above.

Often loud and louder still
With meaning silent they pass unheard
Except to make us drowsy feel
Like sweet ambrosia from up above.

Like drops that fall and patter the roofs
Those songs still louder come
Even noisier than those charging hoofs
Of angels come to oil their cords.

Like waves from space they come to us
Spiraling through halls that resonance add
As notes which like echoes are tossed
Deliciously into ears that hear.

This symphony of celestial songs unknown
Music to the ears of all that hear.
Come to us like tracts unknown
Which we wish will never end.

Dreams and fancies these could be
Sounds mellowed by acoustic walls.
Dreams and fancies reality had been
As we hear those untempered cords.

What sounds formed yet unformed
Do come into our wearied ears
How these choirs in harmony perform
To send our senses to eternal bliss.

Nascent from there those throats refresh
As anthems they chant with pomp and zest
As sweet and honeyed they come afresh
Singing with ease and unhindered zest.

Full and sweet in glorious ease
The choirs stand and sing alone;
Singing of love with ceaseless ease
In praise of He that lives above.

As all this was going on, Johnny was concentrating on what he was writing. Joy on her part had one hand in his pants. That was the beauty of the drive through church. One could sit in his car and do what he felt like doing while the pastor would be there preaching to ears that will never hear nor care about what he said.

By the time the service was over, Johnny's underpants were already wet. The wetness had unfortunately soaked out to stain his pants and so they had to drive straight home for him to take care of that. They jested and joked about that on their way home.

While at home, they tried to recall what the preacher had said but it was all to no avail. None of them could remember what it was all about. They were both there in body, but their spirits were far away. They did not see anything wrong with that since, to them, that was the basic character of contemporary religion.

They were both at home and it was therefore obvious that they were going to take care of other matters. It might be better to leave it at that!

Very early the following morning, they got up and packed their few belongings into the trunk of the car, and they were off. They had taken off towards the west, but they had no particular destination in mind. It was going to be just an open adventure.

When they stepped outside, the first thing that struck them was the beauty of the whole place. The morning was still too young and it was still half-light. There wasn't enough light for any shadows to be cast yet, but it was so beautiful that their minds were filled with love, not just for each other, but for nature as well. The well-mown grass around the hotel was of the carpet grass variety and it felt as soft as Persian carpets, apart from being lush green. It was enough to attract man and animals alike.

With this subdued light came the very thin mist that was around that morning. It only reminded Johnny of the very first time that he had set eyes on Joy. She was also probably having the same thoughts as they suddenly looked at each other. In other words they just stood there and fed their eyes on the beauty of an early spring morning. Everything was calm, smooth and mellow. The leaves were in various shades of green and there was little to no pollen in the air. A few early dispersing trees had already let off their seeds and a few of them had parachuted down. Some had their own parachutes while others had wings with which they flew down from the top of the trees.

The sun had not yet fully come up and the reptiles were not yet out to warm up their blood, scaly skins and bodies as a whole. Only these two lovers seem to be out there yet. They were there admiring each other while imbibing the bounties and beauties of nature. It made them appreciate more the handwork of the creator above.

It would have still been very silent that early if not for a few early birds that just started to pipe their songs. It was more like an unravished quietude that tended to haunt the ears in melodies that could not be heard, and yet were very loud. It was the melody of silence. It infused their speechless companionship with unhindered passion, and if not for those few heedless birds, they had remained afraid to disturb that golden silence.

In the presence of that silence, they were able to sense and feel each other's thoughts, whims and caprices; but it was love that they felt more than any of these. It was like love born out of golden silence and raised into full bloom by that noiseless quietude, which stood as a tiara over its head. This brand of silence tended to speak to their minds in sweet aromatic visitations, and they came in silent caring words, which made them turn around to look at each other once more. This led to a wispy kiss, which in turn became a cue for all the other birds to join in the choruses.

As soon as the sound of that tender smooch broke the silence, a retiring owl let out her final hoot for the night and went in to sleep. It is claimed that the early bird catches the fattest worms, and that must be why there were so many birds that early. A yellow chested white canary piped out her most enticing song. It was in appreciation of the early beauty that nature had presented, but it could have also been because it had never seen a lady who looked as pretty as Joy before then. Johnny was sure that it was singing in praise of Joy.

Many birds had now come to join the fray. Some of them hummed, some fluted and yet one particular bird, maybe a nightingale actually sang. Her song was in praise of the two early lovebirds that stood near that car. They seemed to chatter and gossip about them as they began to fly all around. At least it looked that way to the two of them.

Then came a twittering wren as it flew down and balanced its tiny body on a reed to lap up some dewdrops. She did not exactly stop twittering till she had lapped up a few drops. It was only then that she began to sing in all earnestness and without any effort. The notes came in a trembling voice that was carried through, and reverberated, through the entire area.

That wren sprang from blade to blade and then up a shrub where she sprang from branch to branch. She rendered various songs and each was able to filter down from the trees to their ears. It was at the end of her song that they decided that it was time to move on.

"How I wish that this will never end." It was Joy commenting on the singing birds and the cool weather.

"Me too." That was all Johnny could say.

"Why don't we sit in the car and enjoy it before taking off?"

"I would have agreed with you, but how do you know that it would not make us miss a better one along the road."

"Why is it that I never thought of that?"

"Because they had charmed your soul."

"Don't tell me that you did not feel anything."

"I did. It's just that your voice being more charming than theirs, you actually charmed and snapped me out of it."

"Thanks. Anyway lets hit the road."

"All right." He retorted, and with that they took off towards the unknown.

They had driven for about twenty minutes and it was now broad daylight. Suddenly they passed by a valley that presented such a view that they had to stop to take a second look. The mists had just lost their grip on the valley and their covering hood had just been lifted off. They were driving with the roof down. He felt that the valley looked as lovely as she did while she imagined that it was as pretty as he was. As he slowed down, their minds seemed to be working as one.

The sun was peering from down the horizon and everywhere was much brighter than before. It was for this reason that they stopped and stepped down to take a better look at the fantastic scenery. She stood there and asked him:

"Johnny dear, do you see what I see?"

"The valley?"

"Yes."

"I've never seen anything as beautiful as this before."

"In that case I hope you did not mind my stopping without asking?"

"How could one mind?"

"I just wanted to soak in the beauty of the place. It looks more like what one would expect in paradise."

"It only reminds me of one thing."

"What could that be?"

"You."

"Me?"

"Yes."

"Please knock that off."

"I am actually just thinking aloud. I guess it shows you how I feel?"

She snuggled much closer and gave him a passing kiss. They surveyed the entire place for a few more minutes. It was too much for them. They therefore climbed over the guardrail and went into the valley itself. It smelt very fresh with all sorts of fragrant flowers that were already in full bloom.

It was at that moment that Johnny's mind went on overdrive. He quickly composed a poem about what they were looking at. It was the enchanted mead.

The Enchanted Mead

The darkest hours had slipped through the night
Their mysteries gone with the coming day.
Though but ephemeral to the unseeing eye
Vividly moist and cozy they remain.
I feel safe with these silvery shafts of dawn
With the unfolding mead a scene so bright
Yet electrifyingly cool in the early morn
Having traded in the light for dark.
Shy and careful comes the sun at dawn
To unveil this enchanting charm
Full of flowers that sway unmoored
And heavy from dews that fed their charm.
Oft in waves she rolled at dawn,
As like the fifth it rose and fell—
That soft harbinger of the unfolding day
Full of grace and emotions earned.
What a mead where fancy skips with joy
And happiness seeps through crispy veils
As one feels her anointing plots
In a vale that's some Seraphim's home.
One could see her enchanted lake.
Full of mysteries prior unknown,
Though the heavens do really see
Through those flickers of her celestial dome.

Stuttering and muttering a brook empties here
Calmly happy along her unstressful tracks
Sleepy and languid in fancies real
With naught but a whispery sigh.
Like a newt it silently roars
Though more delicate than the ocean sounds
Or even that embryonic slush that also roars.
In flashy rhythms to calm the fetus.

Noiseless, unthrod her paths appear
Like poetry that silently hoots
As each note in tandem speak
Harried like the notes of a hallowed flute.
A tinkling music as of salvation comes
Which from the air extracts some gasps
As her zephyred weakened winds
Fan through the enchanted trees.
This is angelic music a gift so warm
Intricately wrought as a spiders web
To entangle the soul in pleasurable warmth
And wither her sensations in wearied tones
With very faint strains of solitary 'lute
Yet emphatic in loosing echoes
To extract warmth and passionate affection
That deprives the ego of all her reasons.

This rarified beauty here is nature
Which like imagination fancied stands—
Another romance, a plot of nature.
There to enchant all that dare to look.
Luminous and lovely yet becalming
Neither paranoid nor sleepy in action
Her flamboyant though fancied palm
Calm the fluttering heart with tender passion.

For more one will long in excited plea
Like a milking cow mooing to be milked,
Or like a buckling to approaching twilight
For affections from this enchanted mead.

By the time he snapped back from this trance-like inspiration, they were miraculously seated by the bank of a mumbling brook. Here in the valley there were no humans to see or hear them talk. Dreamy thoughts initiated by this enchanted valley had been distilled free of all thoughts but those of love. The beauty before them was more than enough to produce this effect. These were therefore thoughts of love with an uncaring attitude as their hearts and desires had gotten fully overwhelmed. They had been trapped within this solitude of a single thought. It was the thought of one and only one desire.

Phantoms paraded in their brains to further unleash those wild dreams and thoughts. To them, the dreams were like riding in flight and soaring through the various milky ways. Like a whiff of smoke to a winnowing wind that separates the chaff from the grains, a gust of wind came and went. It helped to isolate these their thoughts further from all the rest.

Oblivious of those birds that watched from up the shrubs and intoned their songs in praise of the early morning, their grandiose delusions in a sort of melancholic dementia, they embarrassingly held tight to each other. Life's various and unwelcome drudgeries had vanished into the thin air, and in full arousal and wildly unhindered movements they tried to grab at each other. It was an unintentional blue print of what was to come.

The fact that they were on the sandy banks of an isolated brook even helped to heighten their erotic inclinations. The brook was music to their ears as it sallied forth from a nearby rock and meandered its whispery way through the reeds and roots. It traced its path with no resistance at all. A couple of hisses could be heard when it flows over a menacing bolder or through some giant intrusive roots. All in all, it was a very lazy brook and that had added to their near impatient lethargy.

The valley was a beauty to behold, but above all was the intriguingly enticing fragrance of various wild flowers. The most abundant were wild lavenders and roses together with lilacs and honeysuckles. It was like that mystical Eden, all relived. A couple of near shadows had started to rear their heads, but like that pair in the religious Garden of Eden, they were there to enjoy and assimilate the beauties around. Furthermore it was their turn to also mess around. It had put ideas into their heads and it was time to taste that forbidden fruit.

It only took for their eyes to meet again before uncontrollable lust consumed each of them. It was unhindered lust. Their minds were already dancing around the remembrance as well as possible enactment of those tectonic activities. The temperature seemed to have falsely dropped as she held him even tighter. The tenderness of that her hug was, as well as that delicacy that came as a kiss, enough to make him begin to caress her all over. He kissed and caressed her all over while she reciprocated in kind.

He finally let one of his palms come down and form a cup over one of her breasts. That marked the beginning of the end. She shuddered while her eyes seemed to shrink backwards. She was there but then she was not there. She was looking at him and yet she could not see him. Her eyes and mind had played a trick on her. They had channeled all her senses and perceptions to what was about to happen.

He kneaded the teat between two fingers and instantly it began to harden and stubbornly push against her silk blouse. She was however kind enough to help them out. She did so by removing the blouse to set them free. A couple of sighs escaped her lips, but they soon changed to hushed and reluctant moans. Johnny took the cue.

He let his fingers slide further down. They settled down when they got to that erotic zone between her legs. She hurriedly fell backwards carrying him with her. He was now on top of her as they lay on the sandy bank. She opened up her legs while her eyes pleaded with him to try and concentrate on that area between her legs. He made sure that he did not disappoint her.

He started off by gently caressing the outer portion of the entire zone. It was already wet with her internal lubricant. Now that the area was fully lubricated, he went ahead to caress, pinch and rub the area more vigorously; She began to moan more loudly. He eventually managed to slip two of his fingers into her inner catacombs. They searched through all the nooks and crannies there in its outer chamber. That made her writhe all around while moaning ever more loudly. As that search went on, another finger continued to rub and caress her miniature erection. The effect of these actions was to make her begin to convulse in a peculiar manner. Her body was already completely wet with sweat when she began to plead with him to let his manhood do its thing. She had pleaded with him a couple of times to "Please put it in", and so he decided to obey.

With a steady hand, he took it and wanted to insert it, but he was wasting too much time. She snatched it from him with shaky hands and inserted it herself. It was achieved in one fluid and fast movement. She had hardly finished inserting it when all his muscles began to contract. He opened his mouth and tied to shout with excitement but not even a sigh could come out. He was now panting wildly. She was panting too. It looked as if they were both off on a panting competition.

Suddenly his ejaculate came pumping out. She moaned loudest now and pleaded with him to let it all out into her. She held him even tighter while lifting up her derrière to let him get further in, while clasping with her legs. She wanted it all, and she wanted it to go in as far and deep as possible. She was now convulsing uncontrollably but they both convulsed in unison. It was wild, but then it was well choreographed. Suddenly she shouted, "Home!" and then collapsed in a heap under him. It was at that exact moment when his ejaculation hit its climax.

It took Johnny a long time to realize what she meant by that word. They had just hit a double home run. As soon as they recovered a little bit of their breathe, they rolled into the shallow brook and washed up. It was unexpectedly very warm and very refreshing. They dressed up and headed back to the car.

Johnny was the first to break the silence:

"Darling?"

"Yes?"

"Are you sure that we are not crazy?"

"That's putting it mildly. Its absolute madness,"

"In that case I will always love to be mad." She laughed at that before asking:

""Why don't you try and be more serious?"

"Because I have never loved anyone, not even myself, as much as I love you."

She gave him a peck for that and then waited for about a minute before making her own confession:

"If that is how nice madness feels, then I'll join you in it. I totally agree with you."

"Amen!" He replied.

"But I was not praying so why the Amen?"

"Whatever."

Joy had been with him but for a few days, but she could already read him through and through. She knew that all he wanted was to leave that topic alone. None of them talked again till they got back to, entered the car, and then drove off.

As they drove along, the only thing that occupied her mind was that question that she had asked as they went into the car. She had asked him whether he remembered that saying that:

"Love is Blind."

When he answered to the affirmative, she decided to add a little more to and rephrase it:

"If love is blind, then passion is deaf."

When Johnny still agreed with her, she decided to explain what she meant:

"When the blindness of love and the deafness of passion meet together and embrace each other, then absolute madness is the byproduct of such a union."

He had not really thought of her as the philosophical type until then. It had added to how the amount of respect he had for her, and he thought of her as a modern day Aristotle. They did not talk to each other for a few minutes before she asked him:

"Johnny dear, what are you thinking about?"

"Who told you that I was thinking?"

"I can see it on your face."

"I was only thinking of you."

"Oh, thank you darling."

"You're welcome."

"Do you realize that if what we did there by the roadside in that valley is absolute madness, it means that love has destroyed our senses or at least lifted all descent inhibitions from us?"

"What exact inhibitions do you have in mind?"

"For us to do that in full view of the car and any possible passersby meant that we did not mind if those passers by or any other persons there were watching."

"You happen to be very right once again."

"If madness had therefore taken over, then it means that our senses had taken leave of us too."

"No."

"Why not?"

"Because we still remembered what to do when we got there."

"I would have considered that as pure involuntary activity."

"Maybe, maybe not."

"And do you realize that it means that one thing that can never be destroyed is love itself."

"But some people who were in love, at times begin to hate each other."

"To me, all that it means is that love had only moved a little bit to the back stage."

"Well, that might be right."

"It doesn't seem as if you quite agree with me?"

"I do."

"There was a very slight hesitation in your voice and that goes to indicate that you don't quite agree with what I said."

"Why don't we leave that topic the way it is for now?"

"Okay darling." With that, she gave him a peck on the cheek.

The journey went on without further noteworthy incidents till mid afternoon. They had stopped at a gas station to fill up their tank and buy a few snacks. They had asked the attendant what lay ahead of them and he told them that they were not too far away from the sea. The road would sort of end around a harbor.

It will sort of end in a small fishing village, and one would see a lot of fishing boats there. It did not take them too long to get there as expected. He had read of that village in a tourist guide that he found in one of the earlier stations. Within thirty minutes of getting there, they had managed to hire a fast boat to go fishing. The owner of the boat was their guide as well as their pilot. Almost every good-looking boat there was on hire for fishing trips. He was not exactly enthusiastic about angling, but under the present situation, it was a more than welcome sport.

The man had sold them rods, lines, hooks and baits from his supplies. He was the owner of the biggest recreational fishing outfit there. He took them to a quiet area around a river estuary. There he turned off the boats engine and let it float around. It was time for the sport to begin.

It did not take long from when they started to cast their lines before the fishes began to bite. They could see and feel their corks bob up and down, then Joy had her own dragged down into the water. Sudden excitement took over as she struggled to reel in whatever was there. When she reeled it in, it turned out to be a six pounder. It was a big salmon, which did not matter to her anyway. She did not really know which was which. To her a fish is a fish.

The catch was however tossed back into the sea. This was because, according to their guide, no one was allowed to catch any salmon during that season. It was spawning season for them and the government was regulating it.

Within an hour, each of them had caught at least fifteen fish. It was unbelievable. They were everywhere and they bite like mad. All the fish that they caught were released back into the water except for one. It was only then that their pilot suggested that it was time for them to join the other anglers further into the sea. That was exactly what they did.

When they got further offshore, they found out that it was there that most of the boats were. It was getting more exciting. It did not take any time at all before something bizarre happened. As soon as Joy cast her line into the sea, something immediately swallowed her hook, together with the small fish that she had put there as bait. Whatever it was must have been very powerful. It unwound the entire reel and pulled their boat along with it further off into the sea. Johnny was convinced that if it was not a shark, then it might be a whale. He shouted at her to let go of the rod, but the pilot was already there and he would not have that. He had already taken over.

It was too powerful to reel in. Another boat then sped to their back and got its anchor roap tied to their boat. It then took off in the opposite direction. That was how they managed to start moving backwards towards the shore, still holding on to their catch. Many of the other boaters had now crowded then and kept them company as they towed whatever it was back to shore. The three of them at times joined together to try and reel it in, but it was not easy. Once in a while, they will see part of its fins break surface but it preferred to remain under the surface.

It was not until they got very close to the shore that they were able to identify it. It was a giant Tuna fish. They felt that it must have missed its way in the sea and come too close to shore. It swam very fast and it was all of ten feet long and huge. All the other boats and anglers had come around to give a helping hand. Eventually they were able to get it stranded on the sands with many of the men inside the water.

When they eventually pulled it out to the land, it turned out to be one of those humongous fishes. No one had ever heard of, not to talk of seen, such a big tuna fish. It could have weighed near to a ton, and could easily make it into the Guinness book of records. News does spread fast. The harbor was already crowded as people gathered around for photographs. These were not just the photographs of the Giant fish, but many had to take photographs with it. It made each and every one of them look like a dwarf.

By then a couple of Iron Chefs and businessman had turned up. Each person wanted to buy the fish. The Cashes were regarded as heroes there. They had declared that since they were all there for sports, if the fish is sold the proceeds would go to everyone there. They had started to call them JJ for Johnny and Joy.

Another person there however came up with an idea that they all could identify with. He wanted them to deposit the proceeds with the only hotel they had there. Some wanted to know why it should be that way when the hotel owner was not even in town. All he wanted was an all night party where each person could drink and eat all he could. It was to be for the entire town. This was unanimously agreed to and the Cashes checked into the hotel for the night.

Needless to describe what took place in that fishing village or town that night, except to point out that it was exactly an all night party as planned. It had attracted every adult in the village. It was not until four in the morning that the two honeymooners were able to retire for what was left of the night.

The hotel was quite a small one. It had only fifteen rooms, but even then, only five were occupied. They had checked into one of the double rooms that were upstairs. It was unexpectedly very cozy. Johnny asked Joy to go and have her bath first, but she insisted that he should go first since she wanted to rest a little bit before that.

By the time he came back from the bathroom some six minutes later she was already fast asleep on the sofa. To make sure that it was going to be a refreshing nights sleep, he called her up and forced her to go for her own shower.

Within ten minutes she was out of the showers and she was more than wide-awake. The refreshingly hot water from the shower had snapped her back into full alert.

"What a day!" She shouted as she came out.

"I am sure I will sleep through an entire forty-eight hours before being able to open my eyes."

"Me too." She replied.

"What surprises me is the fact that I don't seem drunk, not minding how much alcohol I had let into my system."

"Don't you know why?"

"No, I don't."

"It is because we were frantically dancing around all night long. The alcohol must have gone with the sweat. Apart from that, there were lots of oily food there and it is claimed that oil has a way of getting alcohol out of the system. I am not sure of how that happens, but some claim that oil emulsifies alcohol and at times that slows down absorption and so its power to intoxicate."

"Is that scientifically proven?"

"Maybe, maybe not. I have never tried to find that out."

"I didn't think it was, but then it sounds as if it could be true."

"I however know it to be so from practical experience."

"I can see that you no longer feel sleepy."

"Sleep has just run away from me."

"I have never felt more awake than I feel now."

"Come nearer let me show you something."

"What?"

"Please obey before complaint. Just come."

She was seated on the edge of the bed. She had suddenly started dressing up without any explanation, before changing her mind. She had asked him to help her unhook her Bra from behind. The hook was stuck in the eye. He helped her do that, but as would be expected, it also led to something else. All it required was one single smooth motion and it was on the ground.

"You seem to be an expert at that Johnny." She commented.

Without replying he had already helped her up to her feet and then further helped her remove whatever dress she had just put on.

"I can see that you are not a man of many words tonight. I have always admired men of action and I can see that you are one of them. Incidentally I can notice that you are getting very hard." She had said this, as she looked further down towards his legs.

It was only then that he spoke and it was a short decisive statement that was let out to convey some meaning. It was a pregnant statement. It was a short statement from the Shakespearian play, Julius Caesar.

"I have come to burry Caesar not to praise him."

That was Mac Anthony, and she knew exactly what he meant and she also felt the same way too. This was however not a time that calls for speeches. It was a time for action.

As if it was a miracle, he was suddenly naked. It was now a cloudless night, and the only light in the room came from those silvery shafts that filtered into the room from the moon. It had filled the room with a limited and subdued cadence. It was a perfect setup for lovemaking. Their bodies looked more like shadows as they surveyed each other and then began to grope wildly at each other.

It was not long before he went for those breasts. It was the initial trigger. She immediately bent forwards and at the same time backwards in such a manner as to further offer them to him. That was what he wanted and he immediately began to caress and squeeze them. He soon advanced to sucking them while teasing the teats with his teeth. She moaned, she wriggled and she writhed. Now it was time for her to make her own statement. She had sort of re-paraphrased his former statement:

"Please hurry darling. I have come and I am itching to have Caesar buried and not to beat about the bush."

He got the message. He then gently let her down on the bed though hurriedly, and quickly positioned himself on top of her. She was gyrating wildly and moaning, but he was taken by surprise when she exclaimed with a flinch:

"Oops!!"

He recoiled lightly but then he continued with what he was doing. That exclamation had been let out when he pinched her now very hard feminine manhood. It had come to become her dominant hot spot and center of gravity, as it were.

He rubbed, caressed and probed into her wetness as she moaned the more. She giggled at the same time and also spoke a few of those phrases that she had learnt from the land of the spirits. In other words she was once more beginning to speak in unknown tongues.

He was wasting too much time, and so with shaky fingers she grabbed it from him and had it buried within her in a hurry. As she did so she shouted in excitement. It was not that she did not like the fore play, but she was afraid that she might faint from overexcitement. Though he was not fully aware of it, she had already had a couple of very beautiful orgasms.

Suddenly she began to shout while kicking her legs wildly into the air. She gyrated without control. Johnny on his part was also about to loose control. He had that premonition that something big was about to happen—something exciting. That was when all his muscles began to tighten and stiffen. She sensed it and held him ever so tighter to herself while making every possible effort to let him in as deep as possible into her.

Suddenly, he began to gasp and jerk uncontrollably. His ejaculate began to squirt out and deep into her in batches. He was almost sure that they came out of him with supersonic speed and she accepted them as they shot their ways right up into her womb. She welcomed the ejaculate while at the same time being puzzled at how much of it was being released. It seemed as if it was never going to end and that triggered her off once more. She began to quiver once more while gyrating in every given direction as her orifice tightened and loosened its grip around him in waves that she could not tell how they arose.

By now sweat was cascading down from each of them. The whole thing then ended as suddenly as it had started. It ended with a well-synchronized shout followed by a surrendering sigh of relief.

It was a tedious and tiring day and the night had passed so fast that they did not even know that it was already another day. Their early morning bedmatic activity did not help matters either. It had sapped their energy so much so that they had fallen asleep, literarily just before it ended. When they got up, it was just like a short and restive nap. It was not until they looked at the clock that they realized that it was already three o'clock in the evening. Incidentally most of the villagers were still fast asleep. It was time to move on.

It had rained in the night or rather early morning when they were all asleep. The sky was clear of any significant clouds while the humidity was a little bit on the high side. It was a near perfect weather for one to be outside if not for the fact that there was still a lot of water and haze in the air. The sun was up and it was at that moment that the famed covenant arc shot across the skies. There had been many stories as to the origin of that arc or rainbow.

To the Christians and other Judeo related religions, it was a sign of the covenant that God made to mankind. It after he had destroyed the world the first time and let Noah and his family survive. It was a sign of the promise that He had made that He will never destroy the world again with flood. Many did not fail to point out that all that meant was that the next destruction would be by fire. One preacher actually nearly pointed out that the source of that fire was going to be the nuclear bomb.

Others had it that after the fall of the angels in biblical times, their off springs became the giants. The first of these off springs had turned out by coincidence to answer Nimrod. Nimrod also turned out to be a great hunter and it was when he let out his bow to kill a mammoth about halfway across the globe that his fiery arrow traced that path—the rainbow. Many had claimed that the rainbow was actually his bow, and that he only let us see it once in a while where it was hung from up in the skies after his death.

He was claimed to have been the tallest of the giants and that his head actually touched the clouds.

However it happened did not really matter. What mattered was that joy looked resplendent and heavenly in her new dress as she stood by the window to admire the rainbow that had just shot across the sky. The dress was crafted in colors that matched the colors of the rainbow. On the lapel was the monogram: ROY G BIV. That was the name for that design and it was coined from the first letters of the colors of the rainbow. Initially they had believed that it was the name of the designer, but it was not. That had however come to usurp his actual name. It was so designed that each color imperceptibly and miraculously merged with the next.

It was not easy to describe or classify the dress. From the outside it was definitely skirt and blouse, but on the inside it was a continuous dress.

The lapel to the blouse was of a red color but it was not particularly red. It was that shade of red that was mellow to the eyes. It made any eyes that beheld it feel completely at ease. This was followed by an orange band, which led to just below her breasts before the yellow. The yellow looked as if it had just leeched out of the orange above it, or maybe even from the green that followed.

It was an ambiguous green, but it was hard to decipher how it managed to merge and blend into the following dazzling blue. It was the type of dazzling blue that one would expect to find around the neck area of some humming birds or kingfishers. The green had marked the boundary between the blouse and the mid-length skirt while being part of each. That dazzling blue was the first true color of the skirt.

The wide blue band finally meandered its way through an invitingly indeterminate indigo into a wide and vibrant violet hem. The skirt was multi-pleated and the hem was where the pleats terminated and it had a small flare there.

Johnny stood there stunned! Joy was beautiful but that dress turned out to be the exact color and shade of the rainbow that she was admiring. He admired each of them and he was not sure of what to think of her. Maybe she was already up in the skies with that rainbow and he thought of her as a heavenly creature. The only difference between her dress and that of the rainbow is that the dress had colors with a slightly better resolution. He instantly knew that ROY G BIV was a talented designer, though he knew that before he picked the dress.

As for the material from which the dress was made, none of them was sure of that. Johnny had claimed that it must have been from the same material from which the dresses for the royal of royals were made. It was neither chiffon nor silk, but of something different, or even something that could have been a combination of both. It was cool and soft to the tough and had that tendency to cling jealously to the body. When it came to its been worn by Joy, it was a joy to behold her. It hung as close as possible to those her curves.

She only made him remember the model that he had come across once before. It was his first time of coming across such a person. She was a model, but above that, she was a beauty in her own rights. She was just shy of five feet ten inches in height and well proportioned for her height. He had, on seeing her, sworn never to try to describe her. It was not that he could not describe her, but he believed that trying to do so would definitely amount to doing injustice to her beauty. He was of the opinion that no words or strings of words, no matter how arranged.

She was a perfect figure eight. At thirty-two: twenty-eight: thirty-two, she was a total knockout. No one could ever beat that. It might seem unbelievably fantastic, but she made it even more so considering her other features. It was this combination that made her stand out. With her high-heeled stilettos, she was a bit clear of six feet and that made her a spectacle amongst the rest.

Johnny had always adored black hairs and hers were naturally jet black and shiny. They came down to her shoulders in indeterminate coiffeurs that limply hung down like newly emergent corn frills. The barely imperceptible waves of her hair as she walked the runway made one think of various hills and hillocks between which brooks and rivulets meandered their ways down. This was the crowning jewel of her head, which was perfectly sized for her body. It was delicately perched on top of a swan-like neck. It was not exactly long like that of a swan, the neck that is, but it was just long enough to make one remember the swan and make it an attention grabbing feature.

As for her face itself, there would be no need for one to try and describe it. It could easily be compared to the faces of angels, cherubs or seraphs, though he had not seen any of them yet. He was sure that she had a face that was a complete fusion of all those three together. He preferred to leave it at that. At times he was not too sure that it was not his eyes that were deceiving him, since it was at times claimed that beauty was in the eyes of he who beheld. She had at least left an indelible impression on him. Those heavenly beings were claimed to be white, but she beat them in being black!

As for her legs, any leg fetish would definitely go bananas for them. They were simply perfectly sized and shaped for her height, and as for those high-heeled shoes, they made them even more attractive.

All in all, she was an epitome of physical perfection, the model that is, but Joy looked even more perfect in that her ROY G BIV attire. It was already afternoon, if one could remember, and they were already planning ahead on where to move to next, or maybe go shopping in the nearby town. Her sight there had however set that fire burning fiercely once more within him.

There was one funny problem though. Once in a while the thought would cross his mind. Though they had come across each other but for only a short length of time, he was already thinking of what would happen to him if she left him. It was claimed that eighty percent of marriages ended in divorce, often for no apparent reason and he was already thinking of that. He was so much in love with her that he was sure that it would drive him insane. The agony of not being with her would be too much for him to bear. It even crossed his mind that he might probably commit suicide if not that it was against his religious beliefs to do so.

As he imagined, for it was like a waking dream to him, his soul had been wounded. To make matters worse, the whims and caprices of the aspirations of an afflicted soul had been dashed to the rocks. He had emotionally hit rock bottom while disappointment and unfulfillment had come to be his only companions.

Lovelorn, he imagines, he had been abandoned and sequestered to that realm of forlorn beings. He felt like chaff that had been winnowed off and separated from the grains and finally left for and at the mercy of the winds to be blown to the side. Abandoned there and forgotten, he nursed and licked his wounds—wounds that already seemed ingrained in his soul.

Alas, he had been abandoned in time and space to mourn both his lost love and his fate. Life and fate seemed to have conspired to unleash brutality at him. With time however, when that horrendous hold of adversity had begun to ease its grip on him, he began to realize that though life had been bad in that respect, it could always change to the better, even if the better was still bad. He felt that since it could always get better, it might actually change to be good, and that was the basic philosophy behind faith and hope. It was faith in hope for him. It was the hope that he might eventually get over it, even if it was going to take the rest of his natural life.

It will hurt, and it will hurt very badly, even when they stayed apart from each other. He had therefore hatched a plan. For now let it be, but later he must have to try and keep as far away from her as possible. He was not sure that he would be able to do that. Any way, as they put it, a man gonna do what a man gotta do. It was a thought that he had to put to the coolers, but it tended to rear its head once in a while. He tried to compare the outcome of that possible scenario with that of one trying to get honey from a hive of wild bees. They could sting him and it will cause a lot of pain, but the reward is there. He would end up with the honey. He then tried to compare it with one loosing a loved one. They were still not the same. In that case, the loved one will be gone forever and in any case that strong feeling would tend to fade a little bit with time. In this case it was going to be something different and maybe in-between since his love was still there though they were not together.

The excruciating pain and near overwhelming pang of the loss of his love would have been more than enough to stir up hatred within him, but then it was true love that was involved. True love had that uncanny ability to smother, if not cover up, untoward feelings. True love happens to be an eternal feeling, and as long as the object of that love is still there, it will remain; at times even stronger than before. It is an everlasting feeling. Incidentally, this is what explains those bizarre situations of overwhelming abuse in relationships where the aggrieved partner inexplicably opts to remain in the relationship.

He knew that he would get hurt and that his heart would experience near intractable pain with indeterminate numbness taking control of his senses and actions. This would not be lethargy because he was only being consumed by his loss; neither would it me melancholy though it would not be far from it. It was however obvious to him that whatever is made is made and cannot be unmade and so he just had to let it be, no matter how hard it was going to be to do so. He could let it go at least to some extent in order to give succor and solace a chance to come in.

That is the way of life. It was complete affection, total attachment, though without knowing why, indeterminable tenderness and soft spot in his heart mingled with a feeling of passionate intimacy, perpetual desire and unstoppable yearning that was the hallmark of his feelings. He was however bound to let it go, for that was the way of life.

Life is full of ups and downs, and so no one ever got all he wanted. It is full of wishes, many of them granted and many others denied. As a respite, it is claimed that there is always a silver lining to every cloud, or that every disappointment COULD BE a blessing in disguise. He did not quite agree with this, but then, he had no choice in this matter. Fate had taken control and weaved one of those its plots! There was no way that anyone could turn back the hands of the clock of time, unless by negative time travel, if that were possible which it is not.

Since it was total committed love that had plagued him, he reasoned at the end that each should be happy in the others happiness, no even if they were no longer together. In other words, if one of them were to be happy, then the other was bound to be happy in the others happiness, for it is happiness that made love what it was. Since he truly loved her, he reasoned and determined to remain happy in her happiness not minding how separate they had come to be or how far apart they now were. That was the philosophy that kept him going.

The more he looked at Joy, the more he saw that model. Though they were totally different from each other especially in regards to all those inconsequential vital statistics; they could have been one and the same person. Paradoxically enough, they really were. Confusing? Well, bear with me.

The physical differences though only mildly obvious were really nothing and may even not be there at all. They were definitely nothing but the products of the figments of his imagination. Despite all those unending twists and turns of the human mind, he was finally able to put the pieces together. They had been like the disarranged pieces of a jig saw puzzle and now those pieces were beginning to fall into place. That model was Joy, and Joy was that model. It was only his fertile imagination that had created her, maybe just to make sure that she was not going to be the person that he was going to miss.

It finally took a peck from Joy herself to snap him back to reality from his trance or waking dream. From the looks on his face, she knew that he was very far away and worried. That was the easiest way to recall him from that other world:

"What have you been thinking of darling?" She asked as she stepped back to continue with her admiration of the rainbow.

"Nothing."

"Nothing?"

"Yeah, nothing."

"Are you sure?"

"Yes."

"You swear?"

"Depends on what I have to swear on."

"On me."

"In that case I have to tell you the truth."

"What was it all about then?"

"About you."

"About me?"

"Yes, about you."

"What about>"

"Nothing in particular."

"What does that mean?"

"Just a couple of free-wheeling thoughts about you."

"What have I done?"

"Nothing."

"Then why were you looking so worried?"

"Just trying to imagine what life would be like without you."

"Why without me?"

"In case I lost you."

"Lost me?"

"Yes."

"How dare you imagine such a scenario?"

"I love you so deeply that I was beginning to worry."

"But you know that could never happen."

"I started worrying once more after reading the morning papers. I came across that section where it was reported that eighty percent of all marriages here ended up in divorce. Many of these were without any explanations. In fact that figure was quoted while they were reporting on the couple that divorced on the way to their honeymoon."

"You sure do have a free-wheeling and fertile imagination."

"In fact I knew that it could never happen."

"Then why were you worried?"

"How will I know?"

"For you information, during our wedding ceremony I was only thinking about you and I never heard a single thing that the Bishop said except one."

"Which was it?"

"I knew that he was telling the truth when he said 'till death do you part'. It was also directly after saying this that he made that statement that included 'to honor and to hold for the rest of your lives'."

"Thanks for that reassurance."

"You are welcome, and I love you."

"I love you too."

Joy knew that she had that effect on him, but then, she was also aware of the fact that he also had that very same effect on her. Her wish, as she stood in front of that window, was that he should come closer to her. She actually yearned for him. She wanted him to come over and at least watch that glorious rainbow with her.

It was just as if they could read each other's thoughts. He did not waste any time as he began to move quietly towards her without uttering a single word. This was the reason why she considered him to be a man of action and not a man of many words and as of now, the action was all that she was interested in.

He tiptoed to behind her and she sensed it. He then slid his muscular arms under hers and clasped them across her stomach. She did not resist since she was actually waiting for that. She then lightly held onto his hands foe a little while before gingerly and surreptitiously directing them upwards towards her breasts. He did not resist as he followed the cue till he had his palms cupped over them. He squeezed lightly and she bent a little bit backwards to fully surrender herself to his embrace. She smiled yearningly into the empty air as well as to the rainbow before commenting:

"Nice rainbow."

"Which rainbow?" He asked.

"I can only see one there."

"I see two."

"Maybe I am blind and cannot see the second one."

"Your dress." She chuckled at that before answering.

"Yes to both of them, especially the dress which was your choice for me."

"Its only now that I have come to appreciate how it looks on you. Now I can view the two rainbows with one by the other, and they both look nice, especially the person in one of them."

"Thanks for that."

"You're welcome."

"What are your plans for today?"

"You."

"Me?"

"Yes."

"And apart from us?"

"No other plan; but what's your own plan?"

"Whatever yours happens to be."

"Then lets go back to bed."

"Okay. But what of after that?"

"For now, I guess it just has to be one thing after the other."

"Okay then."

There was that saying that what happens in Vegas remains in Vegas. For this reason it might be reasonable for one to insist that what happens in the bedroom remains in the bedroom. All one needs to know is that they went in embarrassed, he because he was ramrod stiff with his pants already wet and she because she felt and was very hot with her pants also already wet. What a couple!

It was some three hours later that they came out from the bedroom section of their suite and ready to leave for where they had previously planned to go.

This newly wedded couple had found themselves moving from one interesting adventure to the other, but it was soon going to be over. They had gone through a couple of other adventures before it occurred to them, that Johnny had only seven days more before he was due to get back to work. It was for this reason that they decided to be on their way back, one way or the other.

When they finally left that morning, it was to drive for the entire day. They only stopped to fill up their tank once in a while. They figured that it would take them a little bit less than one and a half days to get home, if not sooner. At the last gas station where they stopped, they were informed that the next big city was probably about an hour away. The biggest landmark to indicate that they were near the place was a cemetery. The attendant did not have to elaborate on that. It was a cemetery that was almost a mile long. It was used to burry those that died during the civil war but it was later used for all others.

Whenever they got to that cemetery, they were to assume that they were within twenty minutes of the city. It was situated there because the cemetery came to be, before the city. They were driving almost parallel to the seashore. They had gotten used to the soft but loud clap of the ocean waves on the cliffs that marked the entire area. They could also see a couple of lazy steams ooze their windy ways towards the sea, but they were not going to be enticed by any of them once more.

Birds of various colors, sizes and types sang away as they slowly drove along. They did not want to miss the beauty that nature was presenting to them. Many of the streams actually seemed to be reluctant to surrender their fresh waters to the briny deeps.

There were now only a few fair weather clouds above, and the sun shyly slid from behind one to the other. This was as it went on its way to retire for the day down and behind the western horizon. More than a few reluctant shadows remained there. They did not want to be relegated to oblivion. They seemed to be protesting their imminent demise as the sun slid away. They were aided by a couple of reluctant wind gusts. These reluctant shadows seemed to have been caught up between the effects of the fast receding sun and the subtler effects of the fast ascending moon. The full moon was by then way up the skies.

A late rooster crowed to announce his retirement for the day. It was also meant to be a knell for the parting daylight. A couple of fireflies were already out with their miniature touch lights, while that famous star spangled canopy had suddenly and miraculously appeared. A few shadows seemed to have lingered on, but these were nothing but the ghosts of shadows that had long left the scene.

A few gusts of wind apparently had stirred the whistling pines and they whispered in hushed tones to announce the appearance of the queen mother moon. Her subdued rays had already searched through all the nooks and crannies around. It was for this reason that the darkness, which had but just arrived, began to sort of melt away.

They had their roof off and were enjoying the cool evening breeze and while driving very slowly along this almost abandoned stretch of road. It was only then that they experienced their first mishap since the journey began. It was as they approached that cemetery that the car suddenly began to develop a little hiccup. It seemed to cough a little bit and then began to slow down. It stopped to accelerate and finally it stopped.

It had stopped exactly around the middle of that vast cemetery and it was around eight in the night. Having been informed as to the exact location of this cemetery, they knew that they were still some twenty minutes driving, away from the town. They were now very close to the town, but then they were still too far away, especially considering the fact that the only way they were to move on was on foot. That was obviously out of the question. The possibility of another car passing by to help them out along this rarely travelled route was also so slim that it was out of the question to even think of it.

As they sat there in the car contemplating on what to do, Johnny once more composed another poem. This was about the cemetery that they were looking at. It was called Saint Paul's Avenue. He had chosen Saint Paul because he reasoned that most of the dead there were Christians, going by the preponderance of crosses on their headstones. If they were Christians, then Saint Paul must have been responsible for their beliefs. He was claimed to be the person who influenced Christianity most.

Saint Paul's Avenue

Saint Paul's Avenue
Tree sequestered and full of shadows—
Shadows that often danced and flipped
To the nippy awakening nights.
How I long to here repose
Where shadows talk their silent talks
And spirits gossip on all that pass,
Cool and off from the humid heat
A haven for all those wandering ghosts.
With neither worries nor thoughts to task their hearts,
Here they rest in sweet repose
In palaces that rather fancied seem.
Here I guess do rest those souls
That wisely chose a becalming spot
Where shadows sing in tones unheard
To lull their ears to close for good.
Man and beasts alike do long to hear
Yet they fail to hear our pals—
The spirits that rest and yawn at will
Fully unheard by our mortal ears.
Oft this silent eloquence tends to go
As distant murmurs of the spirits that float
Around this cemetery at Saint Paul's Avenue
Where forever they call their home.

They had been stranded in the middle of a vast cemetery. Joy was never the type that appreciated a cemetery by day, not to talk of now that its night. She was afraid, though she was not too sure what she was afraid of there. Johnny on his part did not really care about cemeteries. He was of the opinion that ghosts were everywhere and could never be restricted by the walls of a graveyard. It therefore stood to reason that if one were to be afraid of them, then he had to be afraid no matter where he was. Apart from this, ghosts were not physical entities and so they could never do any harm to man. They were probably less harmful than harmless itself. He tried to get her to see with his point of view, but it was all to no avail.

It would be too far for them to try and make it to the town and so the only other viable alternative they had was to sleep in the car. Unfortunately, her car was a bit on the small side, but they had no other choice. The evening was mysteriously getting warmer and more humid, and so Johnny decided to take a stroll into the yard itself.

There was a gravestone that was bigger than the rest very close to the road there. It had a lot of inscriptions on it and so he went over to take a look at the inscriptions. With the aid of his keychain light he tried to read what was written on it. He was one of the most curious types. It turned out to be not just an epitaph but what could be described as an account given by the departing spirit of what he observed at his burial. It was therefore obvious that the man wrote it long before his death. The dead man had signed it. He had titled it: My Departed soul.

My Departed Soul

O'er I moved across the plains unseen
No longer mortal, neither flesh nor blood
But a spirit that one never sees
Save as the ever softly blowing winds.
My trail never stops nor really starts
Reborn to a feature of ever-rising heights
Where questions unanswered go with time
Extricate from the umbilical waves of life.
Gnawing thoughts engulfed in time
As misty images search confused
Through annals from memories already stripped
Scramble as remembrances fully hushed.
My love does ebb so soft and free
In brilliance gone like the fleetly wind
Or like rose petals that though precious go unheeded
Have died as immortal memories gone.
Tears were shed to say goodbye
For joy or good riddance, I know not which
And yet many impatiently stood
To await the booze to come.

Joy, who was afraid of cemeteries, had opted to sit it out in the car. Now that Johnny was strolling nearby in the cemetery, she realized that going in there to be by her husband's side might after all be the better of the two unwelcome alternatives.

"What are you reading there?" She asked, as she got closer to him.

"An epitaph of sorts."

"That looks rather long, if I may say so."

She said this as she got there and then huddled against him, maybe for protection from the ghosts.

"It actually seems to be an account of what the spirit saw as it left the earth."

"Left the earth for where?"

"My guess is that this one must have left for the heavens."

He knew that all she wanted him to confirm was that it was not anywhere near that cemetery.

"Are you insinuating that it is not anywhere near this place then?"

"That's what I have been trying to tell you all along. The spirit leaves the body at death and departs into the spirit world as they put it. It is no longer here. Only the body was buried here. Even then it will have by now disintegrated into nothing. It is for this reason that it often seems puzzling to me, or to figure out why people go to this extent in building these monuments to nothingness."

"If that is the case, then cremation might seem more reasonable."

"Quite correct. I still cannot see the reason for these burial sites."

"I guess it is to help them remember those departed ones."

"Correct as that may be, it is obvious that it has not yet occurred to them that there are far more dead people than are living. Maybe the departed might be well over a thousand times more in population when considered conservatively—more populated than the living, that is."

"I agree with you but what point are you trying to make?"

"If we had a monument for each of the dead since the world began, then the entire earth will not even be enough to accommodate their tombs."

"You have a point there."

Just at that moment an owl hooted from very close by. She held even tighter to him, being afraid of that eerie hoot.

"Don't tell me that you are afraid of owls too?" He asked.

"It feels particularly eerie to listen to an owl hoot from within the cemetery."

"I know what you mean. One might be tempted to associate it with a sound from the spirit of the dead."

"Exactly."

"But you know that it could not be?"

"Yes, but then . . ."

She did not complete that sentence. Her holding onto him very tightly, and his protecting her with one arm around her shoulder was enough to do the trick.

Let the action begin!

It was still full moon and he could see her very well, but it was not bright enough for him to fully appreciate the total beauty of those her delicious eyes. For her sensationally luscious lips, it did not matter so much, since he could always check them out even if they were in the dark. The little he saw was however enough to literarily sweep him off his feet. She was beginning to feel the same way too. Within seconds their heart rates had increased considerably and their hairs were beginning to stand on end in anticipation of what was going to follow.

She was attempting to look upwards into his eyes, but that looked like an invitation for a kiss and so he snatched at the opportunity to deliver one heck of a passionate kiss. There had always been that chemistry between them as she responded in kind. Passion had taken over their senses and that fear of the graveyard that she had was gone in an instant.

In one swift move, his clothes were off and he used them as a mattress over the concrete tomb. By the time he finished making their bed, which was but for an instant, maybe less than five seconds, she was equally naked. She had flung her dress in a hurry to a neighboring tomb. They were each now as naked as they were when they were born, and they looked at each other rather embarrassingly. Though it was just half-light, they enjoyed what they saw.

He did not waste any time before he began to explore her body. She writhed and moaned loudly as he began. She was totally oblivious of the fact that she could be disturbing the spirits of the dead, or at least if that was not so, the birds that nested nearby. He caressed her breasts as their teats began to harden. It was intensely lovely and insanely pleasurable as her moans continued though more deeply now.

Total physical arousal had taken over and created a sense of urgency, which made them fly down to their newly made bed. His fingers went further down and he began to caress her now fully aroused clitoris. Her breathing suddenly became very rapid and shallow. Her muscles were beginning to progressively tighten up. She was no longer there. Her senses had already succeeded in transporting her or rather tossing her into that mysterious wonderland of orgasmic miasma. It had been spontaneous but it came in a series and bouts that made her wriggle around the more.

He was still caressing that dangerous spot when one finger slipped inside and began to tease the internal walls of her vagina. That was more than enough for her. She began to toss around while all her muscles began to contract uncontrollably. With her arms now spread-eagled, she began to grope for and grip the tombstone for support. It was at that very instant that he sensed his own fireworks arrive.

He feverishly and hurriedly removed his finger and replaced it with his manhood. It was a deliberate, sure but rapid penetration for he was in a hurry. She shuddered as it entered and her moans immediately increased both in loudness and frequency. This was because that intense feeling of pleasurable experience was beginning to make her gasp for air.

It was like a volcanic eruption! They both climaxed at the same instant. It was not just like a volcanic eruption, it was a compound type. Each volcano was spewing its lava everywhere. A series of waves of vaginal contractions arrived with the sole intention of sucking him further into her. It was like a suction pump drawing everything in and he felt it. He loved it. He immediately responded as his own came again once more.

Their muscles contracted uncontrollably as they grabbed and held onto each other as tightly as possible. This had continued for a little bit more than a short while. They had experienced a set of powerful and highly sophisticated orgasms. In fact it was a series of orgasms strung together, and for some, it would be a once in a lifetime experience. For these two lovebirds however, it seems to be a normal occurrence.

Because of the excessive demand of energy by this experience, they collapsed into each other's arms.

It was the enchanting sound of those early spring birds that woke them up. They had fallen asleep and they had slept through the night on that tombstone. It was still spring, that season of rebirth, and many of the birds were already up and about collecting materials to use in building new nests or refurbishing old ones. These were however the latecomers to this building industry. The early brooders were already waiting for their eggs to hatch.

They came in many colors and sizes, but what they all had in common here was that they all sang melodiously. Some were actually squeaks, and others squeals but most came as choruses from completely unhindered throats. They were choruses that could lift off the weight of misery from afflicted souls. A couple of them came as warbles and some as mumbles, but one stood out. It was that distinct rendition from a canary.

They were all songs of joy since each seemed to be proclaiming the arrival of a beautiful morning. It was the arrival of this beautiful rendition that awakened them from their deep slumber. The renditions seemed to reverberate from one tomb to another and resonate all through the cemetery. It was already six in the morning.

They found it rather very embarrassing when they noticed that a raven was perched on a tombstone next to them. It was intensely watching them and they could not tell what it had in mind or what it had seen before. It was mainly for that reason that they hurried up with their dressing up. They had been naked on the tombstone all night long.

Yesterday had been an unlucky day, though they had made the best out of it. Their luck was about to change. This was going to be the exact opposite of the previous day and they had the feeling that luck was about to shine on them. They were hardly out to the road when they heard a helicopter engine coming from the east. The pilot had spotted them and he knew that they were stranded. It was a helicopter that belonged to a news station. The pilot touched down and let them tell their story. He arranged for the news organization to take care of their car. He had called for a towing van to take care of that part of it too.

He finally flew them all the way back home. A day later, Joy's car came back from the dealer where the Newsman had taken it. They then drove to Joys place to pick up her belongings and it was a new life for each of them. They were now Mister and Misses Cash.

Many congratulatory messages came as cards sent to Mr. & Mrs. J. J. Cash. A few of his friends made fun of their name. J. J. Cash was shortened to JJC, which some of them pointed out meant Johnny Just Come. They were new to that type of life and they had just come into town.

Johnny Cash has chased after the wind, he had caught up with the wind and he had finally, as it were, bottled up the wind, by getting hitched to it.